# Sister Magic

## Violet Takes the Cake

We think you will also enjoy these books
by Anne Mazer

# Sister Magic

The
AMAZING DAYS
of ABBY HAYES

# Sister Magic
## Violet Takes the Cake

BY ANNE MAZER

ILLUSTRATED BY BILL BROWN

SCHOLASTIC INC.

New York  Toronto  London  Auckland  Sydney
Mexico City  New Delhi  Hong Kong  Buenos Aires

No part of this publication may be reproduced, stored in a retrieval system, or transmitted in any form or by any means, electronic, mechanical, photocopying, recording, or otherwise, without written permission of the publisher. For information regarding permission, write to Scholastic Inc., Attention: Permissions Department, 557 Broadway, New York, NY 10012.

ISBN-13: 978-0-439-87250-8
ISBN-10: 0-439-87250-2

Text copyright © 2008 by Anne Mazer.
Illustrations copyright © 2008 by Scholastic Inc.
All rights reserved. Published by Scholastic Inc.
SCHOLASTIC, LITTLE APPLE, SISTER MAGIC, and associated logos are trademarks and/or registered trademarks of Scholastic Inc.

12 11 10 9 8 7 6 5 4 3 2 1          8 9 10 11 12 13/0

Printed in the U.S.A.                    40
First printing, November 2008

*To Megan Shull: You know why...*

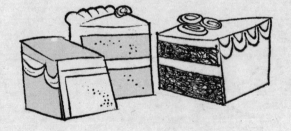

# Chapter One

"I'm ready to leave for the mall," Aunt Dolores announced. "Who's coming with me?"

"*Me!*" Violet yelled. She bounced around the kitchen on a large orange ball.

"Me, too," her older sister, Mabel, said.

Both eight-year-old Mabel and five-year-old Violet were excited. This was no ordinary shopping trip.

Aunt Dolores was getting married to her longtime boyfriend, Howard.

Mabel and Violet were going to be the flower girls in their wedding.

And today they were going to shop for a wedding dress for Aunt Dolores, for dresses for the flower girls, and for other necessary things.

Mabel had never been part of a wedding before. She had never been a flower girl. She had never even seen a bride up close.

She couldn't wait to walk down the aisle, right before the bride. She couldn't wait to wear a lovely new dress and carry a basket of flowers.

She couldn't wait to be part of Aunt Dolores's big day.

Of course, Violet was going to be part of it, too.

That was unfortunate. But it couldn't be helped.

Mabel had worn jeans and a neat button-down shirt for the shopping trip. Her hair was pulled back with two matching barrettes.

In one hand, she carried a small blue bag. In the other, she had a glossy wedding magazine. There was a list taped to the front cover.

"I've been reading up on the latest trends," she said. Mabel had spent hours studying the magazine.

She read from the list. "Layers are in. Pastels are out. Red is the new pink."

"Oh, dear," Aunt Dolores said. "It's so much to remember."

"Don't worry," Mabel said. "I've got most of it in my head, Aunt Dolores. This list is just a memory aid."

"Thank goodness you're coming along," her aunt said. "You'll be a great help."

Mabel beamed. She loved it when people said that.

"I'm here for you," she said.

Violet kept on bouncing. "Hopping and shopping!" she chanted. "Hopping and shopping! I'm ready, too."

Well, Violet was as ready as she ever got.

She wore a striped dress with plaid tights and a short polka-dot jacket.

Mabel shielded her eyes. It hurt to look at her sister.

It hurt to think of the stares and comments they were going to get.

And she wished that Violet would quit acting like a noisy windup toy.

This was a special outing. Didn't she know how to behave?

But Aunt Dolores only smiled at Mabel and Violet. "I'm so excited that you two will be with me today. Think of all the good times we've had together," she said.

Aunt Dolores closed her eyes. "The

picnics, the playgrounds, the water parks, the zoo . . ."

"And I played piano at your engagement party," Mabel reminded her.

Well, it wasn't actually an engagement party. It was really a barbeque. Mabel had played a short concert for their friends and neighbors.

Afterward, Howard and Dolores had made a surprise announcement: They were engaged to be married.

"You played beautifully," Aunt Dolores sighed.

"Remember when *I* played the kazoo at the zoo?" Violet said all of a sudden.

Mabel rolled her eyes. Playing kazoo at the zoo wasn't *at all* the same as playing a concert on a grand piano.

"No one has better nieces than I do," Aunt Dolores said. She glanced at the clock. "It's time to get going, girls."

Violet picked up her purse.

"You're *not* bringing that purse," Mabel said.

"Yes, I am," Violet said.

"Can't you leave it at home?"

Violet folded her arms across it.

The purse was shiny yellow. It had stickers everywhere. It had marker scribbles. It had little stuffed animals glued to its sides.

The purse made people laugh.

It made Mabel blush.

"Aunt Dee!" Mabel pointed at Violet. "She can't go to the mall with *that*!"

But Aunt Dolores only patted Violet's arm. "You look as pretty as a picture."

"The kind of picture that gets hidden in the back of the closet," Mabel said under her breath.

Aunt Dolores tied a silk scarf around her neck. Then she opened the door. "We have a lot to do today, girls."

"I sit behind Aunt Dolores!" Violet raced to the car.

Mabel walked slowly.

She was the older, more mature sister.

She didn't fight over who sat where. She didn't carry hideous purses with stuffed animals glued to the sides. She didn't wear polka dots and plaids in the same outfit.

She was prepared, calm, organized, and very responsible.

One of these days, Aunt Dolores would notice. *Mabel* was a much better niece than Violet.

# Chapter Two

"What do you think about this one, girls?" Aunt Dolores asked. She pulled a wedding gown off the rack and held it up.

The dress was covered with bows and ruffles. It had hoops and sashes. It was shiny and sparkly.

"So lovely," Mabel said.

"It looks like a piece of birthday cake," Violet said.

Mabel frowned at her.

"A birthday cake with lots of gooey, sticky frosting," Violet said.

"It *does* look like a piece of cake," Aunt Dolores admitted.

"Try it on," Mabel urged her. She glanced at her magazine. "Electra Not, the famous musician, wore one just like it at *her* wedding."

Aunt Dolores looked doubtful.

"You never know how it looks until you try it," Mabel said. She had read that in one of the articles. "Give it a chance."

"All right," Aunt Dolores said. She unzipped the last gown she had tried on.

Mabel jumped up from the bench. "I'll hang it up!"

"Thank you, Mabel." Aunt Dolores gave her a grateful smile.

Mabel put the gown on the rack, then returned to the bench next to Violet.

The two sisters sat quietly and waited for Aunt Dolores.

Or rather, Mabel sat quietly.

Violet fidgeted with her yellow purse. She dug through it for some peanut butter crackers.

She took a huge bite and chewed loudly. She smacked her lips and licked her fingers.

Aunt Dolores adjusted the new dress and stared at herself in the mirror. Then she turned to Mabel and Violet. "So?"

"Now you look like a castle," Violet said.

"A castle?" Aunt Dolores frowned. "I don't mind looking like birthday cake. Or a famous musician. But I really don't want to look like a castle. Especially not on my wedding day."

Mabel kicked her little sister. "Violet means that you look like a princess *in* a castle. Right, Violet?"

"No," Violet said. "I mean she looks like a castle. Tall and round."

Aunt Dolores glanced at herself in the mirror. "Unzip me, Mabel," she said. "I don't want flags flying from the parapets."

Mabel jumped up to help. "*I* think you

look like a princess," she said. It was important to stay positive for her aunt.

Aunt Dolores shook her head.

"Don't worry," Mabel reassured her. This was her chance to encourage Aunt Dolores. "There are so many choices. You'll find one that's just right."

"We've been trying on dresses for an hour already," Aunt Dolores said. "I'm starting to lose hope."

It was true.

Aunt Dolores had tried on frilly wedding gowns and plain ones.

She had tried on sleeveless gowns and long-sleeved ones.

She had tried on modern gowns and old-fashioned ones.

The room was full of gowns that looked almost right, were not quite right, or were just plain wrong.

Aunt Dolores looked around the dressing room. "Maybe we should quit for today."

"Just one more," Mabel pleaded. Aunt Dolores couldn't lose hope quite yet. Mabel *had* to be there when she found the perfect gown.

If possible, *Mabel* wanted to be the one who found the perfect gown. Or at least the one who recognized it.

She wanted to hear Aunt Dolores say, "I couldn't have done it without you."

Mabel had spent so much time studying the wedding magazine. It had to count for something!

"What about *this* one?" Violet yanked at one of the wedding gowns.

"Violet!" Mabel cried. "Your hands! Be careful!"

She checked for sticky fingerprints on the shimmering white fabric. Luckily, there were none.

"Try it on," Violet said to Aunt Dolores. "It's the most perfectest one."

"The most *perfect* one," Mabel corrected her. "And it can't be."

Violet knew no more about wedding dresses than she did about computer engineering. She had never even opened a magazine!

"This is the last one for now," Aunt Dolores warned.

She slipped the gown off its hanger and held it up against herself. It was a long white gown with silvery patterns running up and down the length of the dress.

"It's lovely, Violet," Aunt Dolores said.

Mabel had to admit it was. Count on Violet to pick out something gorgeous by sheer luck.

"Funny I didn't see it before," Aunt Dolores said as she stepped into it. "It kind of appeared out of nowhere."

Mabel's stomach did a funny little jump.

*Nowhere?* Now what did that mean? She hoped it wasn't what she thought.

Aunt Dolores smoothed the fabric down around her hips and stared at herself in the mirror.

She smiled in surprise.

"It *is* perfect," she whispered. She glanced at the price tag. "And I can even afford this one."

"I told you!" Violet crowed. "It's the most perfectest one!"

Mabel couldn't say a word. She couldn't even correct Violet's grammar.

Her aunt was right: The gown was stunning. It fit beautifully. It was the very dress they had been searching for.

"Violet," Aunt Dolores said, "how did you find it?"

Violet made a few squiggles in the air with her forefinger. Then she grinned. "Magic," she said.

# Chapter Three

Violet's magic was supposed to be a deep, dark secret.

It ran in the family, but the family kept it quiet. No one liked to mention it. In fact, they barely acknowledged it.

Violet wasn't supposed to use magic in front of other people.

She wasn't supposed to talk about it.

And she *especially* wasn't supposed to use it in front of other people and then talk about it!

Of course, Violet was only five years old. Most kids her age couldn't keep a secret. And they didn't always know how to act in public.

Mabel had done her best to keep reminding her little sister.

When that didn't work, Mabel made up stories, hid things, and even lied to protect Violet and her magic.

She didn't like doing it. But it had to be done. Her mother *couldn't* find out about Violet's magic.

It was bad enough that her mother's little brother, Uncle Vartan, had magic. He'd always been a nuisance because of it, her mother said.

She would be crushed if she knew her own daughter had magic, too. Mabel took her responsibility very seriously.

But all of her efforts had been for nothing.

Her little sister had used her magic to find the wedding gown — and then she had bragged about it!

Mabel had another, terrible thought.

*Perhaps the gown itself is magic.*

In that case, Mabel really had something to worry about.

What if the perfect wedding dress turned into an orange party gown?

What if it decided to grow an extra sleeve in the middle of the ceremony?

What if it turned into a bathing suit? Or a baseball uniform?

Or what if it just plain vanished, leaving Aunt Dolores in a slip at the altar?

"Take it back!" Mabel hissed.

*"What?"*

"That word . . . the one that starts with *m*," Mabel said. "You're only kidding about it, aren't you?"

"No," Violet said. "'I'm not."

On the other side of the dressing room, Aunt Dolores was still smiling as she stepped out of the wedding gown and placed it on a hanger.

Then she pulled her sweater over her head.

Mabel leaned closer to her little sister. "You can't do any magic here!"

"Why not?"

Violet could be *so* infuriating.

"Do you want to ruin the wedding?" Mabel said under her breath. "Do you want to see Aunt Dolores cry when her elegant wedding dress turns into a plaid flannel nightgown? Or a pile of newspapers?"

Violet shrugged. "It won't."

"You're only five! How do you know?"

Violet didn't answer. Instead she picked up her crazy yellow purse and swung it around her head. One of the stuffed animals flew off and hit the mirror.

"Ha-ha!" Violet cried.

Mabel jumped up to get it. Really, her little sister was impossible.

Aunt Dolores's head emerged from her sweater. "What were you saying?" she asked.

"Violet was making a joke," Mabel said quickly.

"Ha-ha," Violet said again.

"Here's your stuffed animal." Mabel dropped the striped creature into Violet's lap. "You can glue it back on your purse later."

She waggled her eyebrows at her sister. She hoped that Violet understood eyebrow language.

*We'll talk about magic later*, Mabel mouthed just in case she didn't. *But not in front of Aunt Dolores*.

Mabel wondered, though, if Dolores already knew about the family magic. She *had* to know about Uncle Vartan.

After all, he was her younger brother, too.

Aunt Dolores also probably knew how much Mabel and Violet's mother hated magic. She might even have a clue about Violet.

Maybe all these "secrets" weren't *really* secrets.

Maybe Mabel should speak to her aunt right now.

Maybe she ought to warn her about Violet and her magic. Maybe it was time to speak the truth.

"Aunt Dee," Mabel began.

"What is it, sweetie?" Aunt Dolores asked.

Her mother's face flashed in front of Mabel's eyes. She remembered how upset her mother had been when Mabel had discovered Uncle Vartan's magic.

What if Aunt Dolores started to cry? What if the news ruined her day? Or her wedding? Or her life?

Mabel just couldn't do it. Aunt Dolores's future was in her hands! She would just have to find a way to keep a lid on Violet until the wedding was over.

It was much harder than being a flower girl, but Mabel was up to the task.

"Um . . . when's lunch?" Mabel asked.

"Soon," her aunt promised.

Mabel sighed deeply. Telling the truth was way too risky.

# Chapter Four

"I'll take this dress," Aunt Dolores said to the saleslady. She handed over the wedding gown and her credit card.

"Do you need anything else?" the saleslady asked. "Shoes? Stockings? Gloves? A veil?"

"No, thank you," Aunt Dolores said. "We're all set."

The saleslady held up the gown.

"This is a lovely one," she said. "It must have just come in. I don't remember seeing it before."

Mabel's stomach did another one of those funny little jumps.

Fortunately, Aunt Dolores didn't seem

to be paying attention. She flipped through a bridal magazine on the counter.

"Look at these." She showed Mabel and Violet a picture of wedding bouquets. "Which ones do you girls like best?"

"The orange and yellow and red flowers," Violet said.

"*Way* too bright," Mabel said. "I like the pale pink ones."

"With that dress, I'd go for something quiet," the saleslady said.

"See?" Mabel said to Violet. "*I'm* older and wiser." It didn't hurt to remind Violet of the facts once in a while.

"But you should pick whatever flowers you want." The saleslady handed the credit card receipt to Aunt Dolores. "All the rules are off these days."

Violet stuck her tongue out at Mabel. "See? *I'm* shorter and smarter."

"Don't bicker, girls." Aunt Dolores signed the receipt.

"*I'm* not bickering," Mabel muttered.

"I don't know what to do about the flowers," Aunt Dolores said.

"Take your time," Mabel said. It was what her father always said when she had a decision to make. "Think it over."

"The only thing I'm one hundred percent sure about is the dress," Aunt Dolores said. "It's absolutely perfect.

"And Howard, too, of course," she added. "My future husband."

"He's what's really important," the saleslady said as she wrapped the dress in pale gold tissue paper. "Some brides forget that."

"Is it time for lunch?" Violet interrupted the grown-up talk.

Aunt Dolores nodded. "We'll have a good lunch together," she said. "And then we'll order some more things for the wedding."

"Like the cake and the invitations and the centerpieces?" Mabel said eagerly. She had researched them all. Here was a place she could shine.

"You have it all figured out, Mabel."

Mabel looked down modestly.

"I hope you won't be disappointed," her aunt continued. "It's going to be a simple wedding."

"How simple?" Mabel asked. "You *are* going to have music, aren't you? And guests? And the walk down the aisle?"

"Don't worry; we'll have all of that." Aunt Dolores added, "And a bride and groom, of course."

"Here it is." The saleslady handed Aunt Dolores a large white box tied with a rose-colored ribbon. "Let us know if you need any adjustments to the dress."

"It fits perfectly," Aunt Dolores said.

"You're very lucky," the saleslady said. "That almost never happens."

Mabel's stomach jiggled again. She was starting to feel like she had swallowed jumping beans.

But Aunt Dolores suspected nothing.

"You girls were such a help," she said to Mabel and Violet. "I don't know what I would have done without you."

This was what Mabel had been waiting to hear.

But *she* had barely done anything. Violet had done it all.

Violet's magic made Mabel very nervous.

So far, it hadn't hurt anything. But that could change at any moment. Who knew what a mischievous five-year-old with magic powers might do?

Violet might make birds fly out of the best man's tuxedo.

She might turn the flowers into fire-crackers.

She might change Aunt Dolores's bridal veil into a shower curtain. Tropical fish might swim around the bride's head.

Mabel would have to make sure that none of that happened. She would have to stop Violet from . . . well, being Violet.

It would be tough, but Mabel was up to the challenge. She would do it for Aunt Dolores.

It was sad, though, that Aunt Dolores could never know what Mabel had done for her.

# Chapter Five

All during lunch, Violet was very quiet.
She ate a grilled cheese sandwich with
tomatoes and drank a glass of chocolate milk.

She had a fudge brownie for dessert
with a scoop of pistachio ice cream.

She said "please" and "thank you" at all
the right times and even wiped her face
with a napkin when she was done.

And she didn't do *any* magic at all. Not
even when the waitress gave them sweet
pickles instead of dill.

By the time they got to the shoe store,
Mabel was starting to relax.

Aunt Dolores was looking for a pair of pointy-toed, silver high heels to go with the wedding dress.

She thought that Sassy Shoes was the place to find them.

But although there were pointy-toed high heels in rose, turquoise, emerald green, glitter gold, and orange, there was no pair in silver.

"We've struck out," Aunt Dolores finally said. "It's time to try someplace else."

They picked up their packages and headed for the exit. Only Violet lagged behind.

"Violet!" Mabel called. She turned to see what her sister was doing.

She was scowling at a pair of chunky white sneakers.

"What did those sneakers do to you?" Mabel was about to say.

Suddenly she realized what was happening.

Violet waved her hand. The sneakers turned into a pair of pointy-toed, silver high heels.

Before Mabel could say a word, Violet scooped them up and ran over to Aunt Dolores.

"Found them!" she cried.

Mabel groaned. Aunt Dolores was already kicking off her shoes.

"They fit perfectly," Aunt Dolores said. "Violet, you're the wonder girl. First you found my dress, now my shoes."

Violet looked very smug as they marched into the stationery store.

She pointed at an empty table. Silver pens in burgundy boxes appeared in an elegant display.

She nudged her aunt.

"A gift for the best man!" Aunt Dolores exclaimed. "You have sharp eyes, Violet."

*My eyes are even sharper,* Mabel said to

herself. *And I can see what you're doing, Violet.*

But she couldn't stop her. The magic was happening too swiftly, too smoothly. How did Violet do it? She was only a beginner!

Aunt Dolores picked up a plain wedding invitation. Suddenly it had silver curlicues.

She picked up a photography album. Her name was already engraved on the cover.

"I can't believe how easy this all is," Aunt Dolores exclaimed. "It's as though everything is waiting here for me."

Mabel did manage to stop one bit of magic. In the flower shop, Violet removed all the thorns from the roses.

Mabel made her put them back before the owner noticed.

Then they went to look for flower girl dresses.

"Enough with the magic already!" Mabel hissed to her little sister. "It's too dangerous."

She wanted Aunt Dolores to have a wonderful wedding — but not if Violet's magic was behind it.

Violet only shrugged.

Mabel prayed that they would find their flower girl dresses quickly and get out of the mall.

This *should* have been one of the highlights of their shopping trip, but now Mabel couldn't wait until it was over.

"I want a dress that looks like a cloud," Mabel said as they entered the department store. She imagined herself wrapped up in yards of gauzy, soft fabric. "Or maybe a petal."

"I don't want to look like a dumb cloud or a flower," Violet said. "I want to wear bright red or bright yellow."

"No way am I going to look like a traffic signal!" Mabel said. "Forget about it!"

"Girls, girls," Aunt Dolores said. "We'll find the perfect dress. Everyone will be happy."

But as they went through the racks of fancy party dresses, none of them seemed good enough.

Some had too many ruffles; some had too few.

Some were too grown-up; others were babyish.

Some Mabel disliked; others Violet refused.

"What about this one?" Aunt Dolores said. She held up a dark blue shiny dress. "We have to find *something* we can agree on."

"I like the sleeves," Violet said.

"I like the sash," Mabel said.

Neither Violet nor Mabel liked the color.

"At least try it on," said Aunt Dolores.

She found one in each size. "I'll see if it comes in a better color."

"Rose or pale blue," Mabel said.

"Orange or lime green," Violet said. "Or bright purple."

"I'll see what I can do," Aunt Dolores said with a sigh.

The girls went into the dressing room. They put on the dresses and then stared at their reflection in the mirror.

"Not bad," Mabel said, "except for the color."

"Yeah," Violet agreed. "It's terrible."

The two sisters looked at each other.

"What if . . ." Violet suddenly said.

"No!" Mabel said.

"But I can . . ."

"*Don't*," Mabel said. "You've done more than enough already. Give it a rest."

Violet didn't answer. She lifted an arm. Then she pointed, first at her dress, and then Mabel's.

A current ran through them.

They made a crackling sound like paper.

Bright colors flowed over their surface.

Mabel looked down at her dress. It was no longer dark blue. It was a pale soft rose.

"*Much* better," Violet said in satisfaction. Her dress was a lovely shade of violet. "Don't you think so?"

Mabel ran her hand over the dress. It was *so* beautiful. And Violet's dress was, too.

She had to admit, Violet's magic could come in handy.

"Yes, it's, um, splendid," Mabel said. "But hurry and change it back. Aunt Dolores will be here any minute."

"So?" Violet gazed at herself in the mirror. She put the yellow purse on her arm and strolled up and down the dressing room, admiring herself.

Mabel took a deep breath. But before she could say a word, the curtains parted.

"I found the dress in crimson and dark purple —" Aunt Dolores stopped in mid-sentence.

"Wow," she said. "Those dresses are . . . yes, wow! Where did you find them?"

Violet opened her mouth to speak, but Mabel cut her off.

"In the dressing room," she replied. It was technically the truth.

Violet smirked.

"Do you like them?" Aunt Dolores asked.

This time Violet cut Mabel off. "We *love* them."

"Well, let's buy them," Aunt Dolores said.

Before she gave the dress to Aunt Dolores, Mabel examined it carefully.

She didn't know exactly how magic

worked, but she wanted to make sure that none was lurking in the dress.

She didn't want butterflies to rush out of her sleeves.

Or for her sash to suddenly snap like a whip, or start slithering along the floor.

She didn't want the pockets to empty out by themselves.

"What are you doing?" Aunt Dolores asked.

"Looking for, uh, rips or broken zippers," Mabel said. She hated to lie.

"You don't need to worry. If there's anything wrong with the dresses, we'll bring them back."

Mabel looked at the dress again. It really was her dream dress. Suddenly she saw herself walking down the aisle with Violet.

No, they'd *float* down the aisle in their rose and violet dresses. They'd carry baskets of flowers and hear the guests whispering about how adorable they were.

Aunt Dolores would be so happy. . . .

It was a lovely vision. But it depended on Violet and her magic. And, no matter how Mabel looked at it, that wasn't good at all.

# Chapter Six

Aunt Dolores held open the door of the
bakery and sniffed the air. "Mmmm . . .
Delicious."

"It smells like cookies," Violet said
dreamily.

Mabel went over to the display cases.
Her mouth dropped open.

There were so many different kinds of
wedding cakes: round ones, square ones,
and diamond-shaped ones.

There were cakes decorated with real
flowers and frosted ones. There were short,
fat cakes and tall, towering cakes that
reached almost to the ceiling. There were
cakes in most colors of the rainbow.

There was even a rainbow cake.

"Can we get a bright purple cake for the wedding?" Violet asked.

"No way! It *has* to be white!" Mabel said.

In her magazine, the cakes were almost always white. Once in a while, they were pale violet or rose or yellow. But not often.

"With orange, green, and blue squiggly frosting," Violet said.

"With fresh flowers or a lace design," Mabel said. "Right, Aunt Dolores?"

Aunt Dolores shook her head. "I haven't made up my mind yet."

Violet went up to a plate of cake samples. She grabbed three or four and began stuffing them into her mouth.

"Violet!" Mabel looked around to make sure that no one was watching.

"I left some on the plate," Violet mumbled, her mouth full of cake.

"Which one tastes the best?" Aunt Dolores asked.

"All of them," Violet said. Crumbs spilled out of her mouth.

Mabel frowned. Now, if Aunt Dolores had asked *her* . . . She wasn't going to make a pig of herself, though.

"Look!" Aunt Dolores cried suddenly. She pointed to a three-tier wedding cake. "My dream cake."

Mabel was relieved to see that it was a traditional three-tier cake, frosted in white.

"It's beautiful," she agreed. "Isn't it, Violet?"

Violet nodded. "It looks like a fairy tale," she said.

Aunt Dolores sighed happily.

"But it *would* be better in bright purple," Violet insisted.

"Is the cake big enough to feed all the guests?" Mabel asked. She leafed through the wedding magazine. "I read a story about a cake that was too small. You don't want that to happen to you, Aunt Dee."

"You are the *most* practical child." Her aunt smiled at her.

"What kind of cake are we having?" Violet wiped her mouth with the back of her hand. "Vanilla? Chocolate? Strawberry?"

"Those are ice cream flavors," Mabel said.

Violet shrugged. "Will the cake have little people on it?"

"Little people?" Aunt Dolores looked at Mabel.

"The plastic bride and groom," Mabel explained. "The ones that go on the top of the cake."

"Yes, if we can find them with ice skates," Aunt Dolores said. "That's how Howard and I met."

"Really?" Mabel cried. "That's so romantic!"

"We skated around the rink and fell in love." Aunt Dolores had a dreamy look on her face. "I'm the happiest woman in the world. . . ." She paused to wipe her eyes.

"What do you think of carrot cake?" she asked suddenly.

"Carrot cake?" Mabel said. It might taste good, but it didn't sound elegant enough for a wedding.

"It's Howard's favorite," Aunt Dolores said. "With cream cheese frosting."

Mabel flipped through the pages of her magazine. None of the articles forbade carrot cake, but still, it wasn't usual.

The baker came up to them. "Have a taste of our best red velvet wedding cake," he said to Aunt Dolores. "Brides love it."

Mabel picked up a small cube and nibbled delicately on it. "It's delicious."

Violet snatched several. "Yum!"

Aunt Dolores also took a piece. "This is very good, but . . ."

"You'd prefer chocolate?" the baker asked. "No problem."

"Many modern brides choose chocolate," Mabel said.

"I think I'd really like a carrot cake," Aunt Dolores said firmly. "It's my fiance's favorite."

"We can make a three-tier carrot cake with cream cheese frosting," the baker offered. "It will look traditional, but your guests will be surprised."

It *was* her beloved aunt's wedding, Mabel told herself firmly. If Aunt Dolores wanted carrot cake, she should have it.

"Can I have it made up like that one?"

Aunt Dolores pointed to the cake she liked.

"No problem!" The baker wrote down the date, time, and place of the wedding.

"We'll have your cake ready on your wedding day," he said. "It'll be just as you ordered. You're the bride. Don't worry about anything."

# Chapter Seven

It was a few days before the wedding.

The food and drinks were ordered, the hall was rented, and the guest list was set.

Everything was organized. Everything was planned. Everything was under control.

Aunt Dolores and Howard were happy.

Mabel's mother and father were happy.

Violet was happy, too.

But most of all, Mabel was happy.

Every day, she dreamed about the wedding.

She imagined herself and Violet scattering rose petals as they walked down the aisle.

She imagined the look of joy on her favorite aunt's face as Howard slipped the ring on her finger.

She imagined Dolores and Howard cutting into the three-tier white cake decorated with roses.

Mabel was happy that everything was going so well for Aunt Dolores and Howard.

And she had to admit that Violet's magic had helped a lot.

Without Violet's magic, they would have spent much, much more time shopping at the mall.

They'd have spent days looking for just the right gown.

They would have had sore feet and tired eyes.

Someone would have cried.

And they *still* might not have found what they were looking for.

\*     \*     \*

Now, weeks later, the dresses and the wedding gown were still perfect.

Aunt Dolores's wedding gown hadn't turned into a pumpkin, pajamas, or a police uniform.

Their flower girl dresses hadn't changed into flowers. Or weeds. Or dark blue dresses again.

Violet's magic hadn't ruined the dresses.

It hadn't spoiled the wedding.

It hadn't caused a single problem.

It was really the opposite.

And the best part was that no one knew. Except Mabel. And she tried to keep it at the back of her mind.

Now the two sisters sat at the dining room table. They were making place cards for the wedding.

They had everything they needed.

Aunt Dolores had given them the guest

list, packages of blank place cards, new markers, and glitter pens.

The two sisters divided up the work.

Mabel wrote the name of each guest on the front of the card. She used her best fancy handwriting.

Then she gave the card to Violet.

Violet drew turquoise hearts around the edge of the place card. She filled them in with bright pink glitter.

"Good work, Violet," Mabel said. "Aunt Dolores is going to love them."

Their mother was going to be thrilled, too, when she saw how nicely Mabel and Violet were getting along today.

Violet finished another couple of place cards. Then she lined them up on the table.

"Did you make one for Uncle Vartan?" Mabel asked.

Violet nodded.

"Good," Mabel said. She had found his name on the guest list. It had a question mark after it.

She didn't know what that question mark meant. Was he coming or not?

She'd have to ask Aunt Dolores later.

She hoped that Uncle Vartan would show up for the wedding of his older sister. But he was unpredictable. Like Violet. That was what made Mabel nervous about magic. . . .

Mabel picked up a fresh place card and began to write another name on it. But she couldn't keep her hand steady.

Was it wedding nerves?

No, something — or some*one* — was making the table shake.

"Quit kicking the table, Violet."

"I'm not doing anything," Violet protested.

The place cards jumped as if they were electrified.

Mabel looked at her little sister. There hadn't been much magic lately. She hoped that Violet wasn't going to start up again.

"*Violet*," she warned.

The glitter hearts suddenly flared out as if they were on fire. A bright light burst from them.

Mabel threw her hands in front of her eyes and screamed.

Violet snapped her fingers.

The flaming light died down. The table stopped shaking.

Mabel peeked out from behind her fingers.

The place cards lay still on the table, shiny and gleaming.

A miniature portrait of Aunt Dolores and Howard had appeared inside each glitter heart.

The portraits looked just like Dolores and Howard. They were romantic and special.

"Oh, Violet!" Mabel cried.

No five-year-old in the world could draw that well. Unless her name was Violet Picasso. She had really taken things too far.

"Aren't they beautiful?" Violet beamed with pride.

Mabel didn't know what to say.

When Aunt Dolores saw the place cards, she'd see . . . that they were *too* beautiful.

They practically shouted *magic*.

Mabel didn't want to be there when the family discovered Violet's secret.

*Violet* wasn't worried, though.

"I did it! I did it!" she cried, jumping up and down.

"What's going on?" Aunt Dolores asked, hurrying into the room. "Is everything okay?"

Their mother followed right behind. "I heard a scream," she said.

"Nothing's wrong," Mabel said quickly. "Violet and I were playing a game."

She hoped they'd leave now, so she could figure out what to do about the place cards.

But Aunt Dolores had already seen them.

Her eyes lit up. "Wow! These are amazing!"

Their mother picked up one and studied it.

"Incredible," she said. "Did *you* paint these portraits, Mabel?"

"Um . . ." Mabel began.

"*I* did them," Violet announced.

Their mother's eyes widened. "We are *definitely* enrolling you in art class," she said.

"The first lesson's on me," Aunt Dolores said. "I can't believe that our sweet little girl is so talented!"

Mabel closed her eyes. *She* couldn't believe how the adults in her family accepted so many things without question.

Her sister was talented, all right.

But not in the way that they thought.

The phone rang.

Aunt Dolores picked it up.

"Hello?" she said. "Yes, this is . . ."

And then she was silent.

# Chapter Eight

"That was the bakery," Aunt Dolores said as she hung up the phone. Her hands shook a little.

"Is something wrong?" the girls' mother asked. "Do they want to change the color of the icing? Or have they run out of buttermilk?"

"Worse than that." Aunt Dolores took a breath. "They had a fire early this morning. It destroyed their kitchen. Fortunately, no one was hurt."

"But what about your wedding cake?"

"It's toast," Aunt Dolores said sadly.

"I thought it was cake," Violet said. She snickered at her own joke.

"Hush," Mabel said. This was no time to be making jokes. Poor Aunt Dolores!

"Do you think I can find another bakery?" Aunt Dolores asked.

"Three days before the wedding?" Mabel's mother said. "Not likely. How about a sheet cake from the store?"

"I don't want a crummy supermarket cake," Aunt Dolores said. For a moment, she sounded like a little kid.

"Cakes are always crumby," Violet said. "Ha-ha."

Mabel frowned at her.

"What about cheesecake? " their mother asked. "There's a delicious brand in the freezer section. We could put fresh berries on top."

"Howard hates cheesecake," Aunt Dolores said. "Maybe we should skip the cake. Maybe it isn't that important."

"Yes, it is! You *have* to have a cake!" Mabel cried. The bridal magazines all said that it was traditional for the bride and groom to feed each other a slice of cake after they cut it.

But now they would have to feed each other a slice of . . . what? Goat cheese? Butternut squash?

Not romantic at all.

And they wouldn't be able to freeze a slice of wedding cake for their first anniversary, either.

Mabel couldn't bear the thought of it.

"What can I do?" Aunt Dolores cried. "I'm not going to bake the cake myself. I'm a disaster in the kitchen. And besides, I don't have time."

Mabel glanced at Violet.

Their eyes met.

Was her little sister thinking what *she* was thinking?

Why couldn't *they* make a wedding cake for Aunt Dolores? She and Violet could do it.

It was such a brilliant idea that Mabel almost leaped out of her chair.

Then she stopped.

Would their cake be good enough to serve at a wedding?

Mabel remembered the last cake she had made. When it came out of the oven, it had looked like a crater from the moon.

It was delicious, though. And she had filled the holes with whipped cream. No one had complained.

Of course, that was just a plain old dessert, not a wedding cake or even a birthday cake.

But why *couldn't* she bake a wedding cake? Mabel knew how to follow directions. It was what she did best.

She also had a few cooking skills, like measuring and sifting and stirring.

And, besides, if all else failed, there was always Violet's magic.

They might even get away with it. . . .

Neither her mother nor Aunt Dolores had noticed anything funny about the place cards.

Or about the dress, the shoes, the invitations, or anything else . . .

Violet's magic had gone well so far. Why not one final touch?

Mabel wanted her favorite aunt to have a wedding she'd remember for a lifetime.

She didn't want her to settle for a supermarket wedding cake.

It was worth the risk.

"*We* could do it," Mabel blurted out. "Me and Violet, I mean. We could make a cake for you, Aunt Dolores."

Aunt Dolores shook her head. "You've both done so much already. It's too much to ask of a couple of kids."

"No, it isn't," Mabel said.

"We can do it," Violet said.

Mabel grabbed Violet's hand. "Together we're strong," she said.

"And mighty," Violet added.

Their mother frowned. "Never mind about strong and mighty. What about safety?"

"We won't touch the hot oven," Mabel said. "Or use the mixer without an adult nearby."

"We won't," Violet echoed.

Her mother shook her head. "I know you can bake a cake," she said. "I think you'll follow safety rules. But can you really bake a *wedding* cake?"

Mabel looked at Violet.

Violet looked at Mabel.

"Why not?" Mabel said. "I mean, it won't be perfect. But it'll be good."

"And it'll be very pretty," Violet said.

Aunt Dolores nodded. "I'd love a homemade wedding cake," she said. "It'll make my wedding special."

"Are you *sure*?" the girls' mother said.

"Look at these place cards!" Aunt Dolores exclaimed. "There's nothing Mabel and Violet can't do if they put their minds to it."

Violet pumped her fist in the air.

Mabel let out a long sigh.

"I'm going to love whatever these two cook up," Aunt Dolores said.

# Chapter Nine

Mabel went online and found a recipe for a three-tier carrot cake with cream cheese frosting. She printed it out.

She read the instructions three times.

She made sure they had all the ingredients.

She took out baking pans, measuring spoons and cups, whisks, sifters, peelers, bowls, and graters.

She wiped down the counters.

Her mother preheated the oven and got out the mixer.

Mabel had promised not to use them on her own.

But she was going to do everything else by herself.

With Violet's help, of course.

Mabel *loved* having a project with a clear plan.

"You get out the dry ingredients, Violet." Mabel tied an apron around her waist. "That's flour, baking powder, baking soda, salt, spices, and sugar."

She opened the refrigerator. "And I'll get the butter, carrots, raisins, nuts, honey, and eggs."

"Okay, Mabel." Violet opened the cupboard and began to take out bags of flour and sugar, and fragrant spice jars.

As Mabel got out eggs and sticks of butter, she hoped that the finished cake would be beautiful.

But what if the cake didn't turn out perfectly? What if it needed a little help?

Mabel was always asking Violet *not* to do magic. She really couldn't ask her to *do* it now. That would set a bad example.

She hoped that her little sister would figure things out on her own.

After all, no one had asked Violet to use magic on the wedding gown, the shoes, the flower girl dresses, the invitations, or the place cards.

And look how well *they* had turned out!

Mabel hoped that when the cake came out of the oven, Violet would see if it needed a little nudge.

And then her little sister would wave a finger or rub her nose and transform it in the blink of an eye.

Mabel would pretend not to notice. But she would secretly cheer her on.

Mabel set a package of nuts on the counter. She shook her head. She couldn't let herself think like this.

"We *can* do it," she said to herself. "We can bake a cake without magic. We'll just take it step by step. We can do whatever we set our minds to, even if we're kids."

She cut open the top of the bag. "We're

going to make the most fabulous wedding cake for Aunt Dolores," she said to her sister. *"Promise?"*

"Triple pinky swear," Violet said.

"We're on our way!" Mabel began to chop the nuts. She felt as if she were setting out on a grand adventure.

"Can I break the eggs?" Violet asked.

Mabel handed her a stainless steel bowl. "Make sure that no eggshell falls in the bowl."

"Okay, Mabel," Violet said.

She picked up the egg and ran her finger over it. Then she smashed it hard against the edge of the bowl.

Egg and shell dripped onto the counter.

"What are you doing?" Mabel cried.

"I got *almost* all of it in," Violet said.

Mabel grabbed a sponge and wiped up the mess. "Let me show you the right way."

She picked up an egg and tapped it delicately on the edge of the bowl. "See?"

Violet watched her.

"Now you try," Mabel said, handing her another egg.

This time, Violet broke the egg perfectly into the bowl.

"You're a quick learner," Mabel said.

Her little sister beamed with pride.

She cracked more eggs into the bowl.

Each time the shell broke cleanly. Each time a perfect whole egg plopped into the bowl.

Each time not a drop was spilled.

Was that magic?

Or was it Violet?

Mabel couldn't tell.

But she hoped it was a sign.

She hoped that the rest of the cake baking would go as smoothly as this.

# Chapter Ten

By the end of the day, all three cake layers were baked and cooled on racks.

Everything seemed to be going well.

The layers, when they came out of the oven, had been close to perfect.

Sure, Violet had made them spin in the air with her magic. But only for a minute.

And only when no one was in the kitchen.

For once, Mabel was pleased to see Violet doing magic. She hoped that there would be even more of it.

Or did she, really?

*One step at a time*, Mabel told herself. *Don't be so quick to rely on magic! We can do it. Violet and I can bake a three-tier wedding cake* without *supernatural help.*

They began to prepare the icing. First the butter and the cream cheese. Then the confectioner's sugar and the milk.

It was thick and creamy, just like the recipe said.

Mabel and Violet spread the frosting over the cake. They put the layers together and carefully placed fresh flowers around the edges.

Then they put the finished cake inside a glass server.

The two sisters stood back to survey their handiwork.

"It's great!" Violet cried. "Aunt Dolores is going to love it!"

"Really?" Mabel said doubtfully. She squinted at the cake.

It was tall and white and smelled delicious.

The baking had gone so well. But the final result? She didn't know what to make of it.

"It's so pretty-ful."

"That's not a real word, you know."

"*So*?"

Mabel tried looking at the cake from all angles.

She closed one eye, then another.

Then she made up her mind.

"It's horrible," she concluded.

The cake was tall, but it sagged.

The frosting was white, but not a wedding white. It was a sort of gray-white, like a newspaper.

The fresh flowers were already wilting.

The whole thing looked like it was about to keel over.

Mabel had known that the cake was going to look homemade.

But she hadn't thought it would look *this* homemade.

"I wish we could throw this out and start all over," she said fiercely.

"I like it," Violet said in a small voice. "We did a good job."

Mabel let out a long sigh.

The wedding was tomorrow, anyway. There wasn't any time to bake another one.

"Why did we think we could bake a wedding cake?" she asked. This cake looked *nothing* like the cakes in the magazines.

"But we *did*," Violet said.

"It's not good enough for Aunt Dolores," Mabel said.

"I like it," Violet said again, more loudly this time.

"You can make it even better," Mabel hinted. Would Violet get the message?

Her little sister licked some frosting from a spoon.

"Point your finger," Mabel said more boldly. "Light up the frosting. Make the thing glow in the dark. Whatever."

"What?" Violet said.

"*You* know!"

The cake just sat there.

"*Do* something, Violet! Rescue the cake!"

Violet ran over to a desk and took out two small plastic figures of a bride and groom.

Then she plopped them on the top of the cake.

"There!" she said triumphantly. "Now it's perfect."

Mabel looked at the figures in dismay. They looked like the survivors of a boat wreck.

They were sinking slowly into the frosting. By the wedding tomorrow afternoon, they'd be buried.

"Violet, please." Mabel abandoned her pride. "Use your magic. Make this cake look just like the one in the bakery."

There. She had said it. She couldn't make it any clearer than that.

But Violet didn't do it.

She had a stubborn look on her face. Usually she looked like that when Mabel ordered her *not* to do magic.

"Why should I?" Violet demanded.

"Because Howard feeds the cake to Aunt Dolores —" Mabel began.

"Why can't she eat it herself?" Violet interrupted.

"It's part of the wedding," Mabel explained. "The bride and groom feed each other cake. But what if one of them has to spit it out?"

"You *always* have to have things perfect!"

Violet said. "But Aunt Dolores won't care. . . . She'll love the cake because *we* made it."

She went to the door.

"Aunt Dolores!" she called. "Come see your cake! It's all done!"

"No!" Mabel looked for a place to hide the cake.

Too late. Aunt Dolores came into the room.

"Mmmm . . . It smells delicious in here," she said.

And then she caught sight of it.

"I know it's not what you want," Mabel began.

"Oh, but it is," Aunt Dolores said quickly. "I'm so proud to have a cake baked by my favorite nieces."

Violet jumped up and down with excitement. "We baked your cake! All by ourselves!"

Mabel shook her head. She couldn't

believe that her little sister thought that messy, wobbling cake was beautiful.

She couldn't believe that Violet would refuse to use magic on it.

Aunt Dolores was being kind. But Mabel knew the truth.

# Chapter Eleven

It was the day of the wedding.

The guests were all seated.

Howard stood at the altar waiting for his bride.

Mabel and Violet wore their rose and violet flower girl dresses. They each held a basket of rose petals.

Mabel felt as lovely and light as one of the rose petals.

She and Violet stood together at the back of the room, waiting for their moment to walk down the aisle.

"Are you ready?" Mabel whispered.

Violet nodded. Her eyes were huge. She

glanced nervously at all the people in the pews.

"Just hold on to me," Mabel said. "You'll be all right."

She brushed back a strand of Violet's hair.

"Let's go." Mabel took a deep breath and stepped into the aisle.

Hand in hand, the two sisters walked slowly toward the altar.

Mabel felt like she was moving in slow motion. Everyone in the room was watching them.

Next to her, Violet gripped her hand tightly.

"Look at the flower girls!" people exclaimed. "They're so sweet."

"Aren't they precious?"

What would these people say when they saw the wedding cake?

Mabel didn't think they'd say "sweet" or "precious."

She nudged Violet. "It's not too late," she whispered. "You can still rescue the cake."

"I like it the way it is," Violet said. "And so does Aunt Dolores."

"That's what you think," Mabel muttered under her breath.

The opening chords of the wedding march boomed out.

"Please, Violet," Mabel begged under cover of the music. "Don't let her get married with that cake. It's not good enough for her!"

"It *is*," Violet said. "You're wrong."

"*You* are," Mabel retorted.

Violet began to walk more quickly.

"Slow down!" Mabel hissed.

"I want to get to the altar!" Violet shouted.

The wedding guests burst out laughing.

Mabel's face turned bright red.

First the cake, now this.

She glanced at Howard. She hoped he wasn't upset. But he was laughing, too.

They had reached the altar. There was nothing more to say.

Violet let go of Mabel's hand and went to her place.

Aunt Dolores was coming down the aisle.

Right behind her, the air shimmered. Uncle Vartan walked in and took a seat at the back of the hall.

Now the whole family was here. Mabel was happy he had come. And maybe he would help with the cake.

Mabel forgot her worries as Aunt Dolores took Howard's hand. The officiant began to read the words of the service.

People dabbed at their eyes with handkerchiefs.

Mabel looked over at Violet. She was sniffing, too.

Everyone was crying. It was so romantic.

It was all so perfect — except for the cake.

Mabel started to cry, too. Only she was crying for what could have been — if only Violet had helped.

# Chapter Twelve

At the reception, Aunt Dolores waved her bouquet in the air to get everyone's attention.

"I have an announcement," she said. "It's about the cake."

At her side, Howard clapped loudly.

"My wedding cake was lost in a bakery fire. But my wonderful nieces, Mabel and Violet, came in to save the day. They made us one yesterday. They are only eight and five years old.

"Thank you, girls, for the best wedding present ever!"

Everyone burst into applause.

Violet jumped up and down with excitement.

But Mabel looked down at her feet.

"Bring it out," Aunt Dolores told the servers.

Mabel shut her eyes. She wanted this to be over.


The waiters placed the cake on the table.

The guests gasped in awe. Or maybe it was shock. Or even fear.

The cake looked like a ship that was sinking in slow motion.

Or like a gray, mushy avalanche.

The top layer was tilting off the cake. The tiny figures of the bride and groom seemed to be hanging on for dear life.

It was only a matter of time before the entire thing collapsed.

Mabel looked around for Uncle Vartan.

The last time she had seen him, he was blowing his nose into a large lavender handkerchief. But he seemed to have vanished completely.

"It looks awful," a small voice said. "I can help."

Mabel looked down at Violet. *Finally!*

But it was way too late.

"Everyone has already seen the cake," she said, shaking her head. "We're stuck with it."

"But I can fix it," Violet offered.

"I don't want you getting in trouble," Mabel said.

Violet pointed her finger.

"Oh, no, you don't," Mabel said.

She pulled her little sister away.

Aunt Dolores and Howard stepped up to the cake. It was time for them to feed each other the first slice.

Mabel winced as dozens of people took out their digital cameras. Including both her parents.

Flashes went off wildly. And when the

commotion had died down, there was suddenly silence.

There, on the pedestal, was Aunt Dolores's dream wedding cake. It wasn't the cake that had been there only a few seconds earlier.

It was the cake they had seen in the bakery.

The guests rubbed their eyes.

A few people gasped.

Others began to applaud. "Bravo!" they cried, as if they had seen some especially marvelous trick.

Mabel's hand flew to her mouth. How were they going to explain this? And what was Aunt Dolores going to say?

Aunt Dolores looked confused. But then Howard picked up the cake knife. "Shall we begin?" he asked.

Together, the bride and groom sliced into the new, perfect cake.

As Howard offered Aunt Dolores the first

bite, Mabel stepped closer to see what kind of cake it was.

It looked like carrot cake. But this cake's icing was bridal white, not newspaper gray.

And now Mabel noticed, for the first time, that two tiny figures of a bride and groom were skating on top of the cake.

Violet had gotten that right, too.

"Delicious," Aunt Dolores said. She fed a bite to Howard.

"This is one of the best carrot cakes I've ever tasted." He put his arm around his new bride. "And this is the happiest day of my life."

Mabel let out a long breath. Was it possible that things were going to be okay?

"Mabel and Violet!" Aunt Dolores called her two nieces up to the front of the room. "I want you to be the first members of the family to have a piece of wedding cake."

Violet was all smiles as she took her cake from Howard.

"And here's one for our head chef," Howard said. He handed another plate to Mabel.

"Um, well . . ." Mabel began awkwardly. Howard had to know that she hadn't actually baked this masterpiece.

He put his fingers to his lips. "I'm not telling," he whispered.

Mabel stared at him. What did he mean? How much did he know?

Aunt Dolores put her arm around Mabel. "I couldn't have done it without you and Violet."

"I hope you're happy, Aunt Dee," Mabel said.

"Oh, this is my dream wedding," Aunt Dolores said. "Everything has gone much better than I imagined."

*For me, too*, Mabel thought.

Her aunt leaned over to hug one of her friends.

"I love how you switched the cakes," the friend said to Mabel. "Did you put the homemade cake in the refrigerator?"

"Of course they did," Aunt Dolores said. "But I can't figure out how they did it so fast."

"That's, uh, our secret," Mabel said. She hoped her aunt wouldn't question her further.

But Aunt Dolores was too busy handing out cake and hugging people.

Mabel sat down next to Violet. Her little sister had polished off a large slice of cake and was now licking the last few crumbs from the fork.

"It's very good," Mabel said slowly. "You did a good job."

"I did, didn't I?" Violet hopped off her chair. She spread out her arms and twirled in a circle.

"Violet," Mabel said, "you take the cake."

# About the Author

Anne Mazer grew up in a family of writers in upstate New York and remembers waking up every morning to the sounds of two noisy electric typewriters. She loved books so much that she would sometimes read up to ten books in a single day! She is the author of forty books for young readers, including The Amazing Days of Abby Hayes series and the award-winning picture book *The Salamander Room*. To learn more about Anne, visit her at www.AmazingMazer.com.

Author photo by Mollie Futterman

Here's a sneak peek at

# Sister Magic

## Mabel on the Move

BY ANNE MAZER

As the car turned onto their cousins' road, Mabel began to get nervous.

They had lots of exciting things planned for their vacation.

They were going to a lake. They were going to a botanical garden. They were going to sleep in a tent.

But Mabel hadn't seen her cousins for years.

She knew that Zoe liked sports and reading. She played soccer, baseball, lacrosse, and tennis.

What was she like? Was she organized like Mabel? Or messy like Violet?

Was she friendly or stuck-up? Was she energetic or lazy? Shy or social?

What if she and Mabel couldn't stand each other? What if they didn't like doing the same things?

They'd be stuck together for a week. They'd have to make the best of it.

And then there were Mya and Violet.

The last time they had seen each other, they were two years old. They were practically babies.

But now they were in kindergarten.

Mabel hoped that the two five-year-olds would get along. Mya liked gymnastics; Violet liked magic....

Right there was a big problem.

Would Violet keep her magic secret from Mya? Mabel hoped that she had warned her about it strongly enough during "the Talk."

*　　*　　*

"We're here!" her father announced, turning down a tree-lined road.

"Hooray!" Violet yelled. She threw a bunch of candy wrappers into the air. They fluttered down on the seat and floor.

"Violet," Mabel said. "I bet Mya doesn't throw candy wrappers all over the back seat."

Her little sister stuck out her tongue. "You don't know that!"

Ahead of them was a big yellow house. Mabel's stomach began to churn nervously.

"I can't *wait* to get out of this car," their mother said.

"Me, neither," their father said. He turned into the driveway.

"Where's Mya?" Violet asked eagerly. "I want to go swimming with her."

"Tomorrow," their mother promised as the car came to a halt.

As Mabel fumbled with her seat belt, Violet shot out of the car.

The front door opened and two girls rushed from the house to meet them.

The older girl, Zoe, was wearing cutoff jeans and a T-shirt. A baseball cap perched on her head. Her hair was cut short, almost like a boy's.

The younger one was dressed in pink shorts and a frilly top. She was cute and tiny, like a dancer.

She pranced down the driveway and came to a halt in front of Violet. The two five-year-olds stared at each other.

Mya grinned. There was a big gap in the middle of her mouth. "I just lost a tooth," she said to Violet. "Wanna see it?"

She and Violet grasped hands and ran into the house together.

*Oh, dear,* Mabel thought. They hadn't been here for more than a few moments, and already she had broken her vow to keep her eye on Violet.

But Mabel couldn't watch Violet every single second. Could she?

She got out of the car. She and Zoe looked at each other shyly.

Their parents were greeting each other.

"Jerrold!" Mabel's father exclaimed. "Susanna!"

"It's been way too long," Mabel's mother said.

Zoe began to toss a baseball into the air and catch it.

Mabel felt awkward. Should she join in? Or not?

Zoe threw down the baseball. "Come on," she said. She led Mabel into the house.

"This is *my* room," she said proudly, opening a door.

Her room had posters of baseball players and koala bears. There were clothes on the floor and books on the bed.

*It's a mess,* Mabel thought. But she tried to be polite.

"Nice posters," she said. She was glad she didn't have to sleep there.

"Thanks," Zoe said. She led Mabel into the hall again.

"And here's Mya's room." Zoe flung open the door to an even messier room, decorated in pink and white and lavender.

"And here's where you and Violet are going to sleep," she said.

"Me and Violet?" Mabel let out a sigh of relief.

She glanced at the two single beds, made up with plaid blankets. A small shelf held paperback books.

It was clean and neat. And Mabel had her own bed.

"It looks very nice," she said to Zoe.

Zoe sat down on one of the beds. "Are you a good swimmer? Can you swim in deep water?"

"Sure," Mabel said. "I love to swim. We have a pool in our backyard."

That was because of Violet's magic, of course.

# Come flutter by Butterfly Meadow!

**Butterfly Meadow**
*Dazzle's First Day*
by Olivia Moss

**Butterfly Meadow**
*Twinkle Dives In*
by Olivia Moss

**Butterfly Meadow**
*Three Cheers for Mallow*
by Olivia Moss

**Butterfly Meadow**
*Skipper to the Rescue*
by Olivia Moss

# Meet Ruby.

She sings like nobody's business, has a pet iguana, and dreams of being a famous animal doctor!